Cuddled and Carried
Hardback ISBN 13: 978-1-930775-99-2 • ISBN 10: 1-930775-99-7 | First Edition • October 2018
Paperback ISBN 13: 978-1-930775-98-5 • ISBN 10: 1-930775-98-9 | First Edition • October 2018
eBook ISBN 13: 978-1-930775-43-5 • ISBN 10: 1-930775-43-1 | First Edition • October 2018
Part of the Platypus Media collection, Beginnings
Beginnings logo by Hannah Thelen, © 2018 Platypus Media

Written by Dia L. Michels, Text © 2018
Illustrated by Mike Speiser, Illustration © 2018
Painting on page 28 by Jim Fox, Painting © Phoebe Fox, 2018

Project Manager: Anna Cohen, Washington, D.C.
Cover and Book Design: Holly Harper, Blue Bike Communications, Washington, D.C.
        and Linsey Silver, Element 47 Design, Washington, D.C.

Also available in Bilingual (English/Spanish) • First Edition • June 2018
        Hardback ISBN 13: 978-1-930775-96-1 • ISBN 10: 1-930775-96-2
        Paperback ISBN 13: 978-1-930775-95-4 • ISBN 10: 1-930775-95-4
        eBook ISBN 13: 978-1-930775-97-8 • ISBN 10: 1-930775-97-0

Previously published in a condensed edition in February 2016 as
        Nurtured and Nuzzled • Criados y Acariciados
        Paperback ISBN 13: 978-1-930775-80-0 • ISBN 10: 1-930775-80-6
        eBook ISBN 13: 978-1-930775-81-7 • ISBN 10: 1-930775-81-4

Teacher's Guide, available in English and Spanish, at the Educational Resources page of PlatypusMedia.com.

Published by: Platypus Media, LLC
        725 8th Street, SE
        Washington, D.C. 20003
        202-546-1674 • Toll-free 1-877-PLATYPS (1-877-752-8977)
        Info@PlatypusMedia.com • www.PlatypusMedia.com

Distributed to the book trade by: National Book Network
        301-459-3366 • Toll-free: 1-800-787-6859
        CustServ@nbnbooks.com • www.NBNbooks.com

Library of Congress Control Number: 2018939431

10 9 8 7 6 5 4 3 2 1

Printed in Canada.

Dear Reader,

We're excited to introduce you to this wonderful book about animals, part of our Beginnings collection.

Scientific curiosity begins in childhood. Exposure to animals and their environments—whether in nature or in a book—is often at the root of a child's interest in science. Young Jane Goodall loved to observe the wildlife near her home, a passion that inspired her groundbreaking chimpanzee research. Charles Turner, pioneering entomologist, spent hours reading about ants and other insects in the pages of his father's books. Marine biologist, author, and conservationist Rachel Carson began writing stories about squirrels when she was eight. Spark curiosity in a child and watch them develop a lifelong enthusiasm for learning.

These beautifully illustrated, information-packed titles introduce youngsters to the fascinating world of animals, and, by extension, to themselves. They encourage children to make real-world connections that sharpen their analytical skills and give them a head start in STEM (science, technology, engineering, and math). Reading these titles together inspires children to think about how each species matures, what they need to survive, and what their communities look like—whether pride, flock, or family.

More than a simple scientific introduction, these animal stories illustrate and explore caring love across the mammal class. Showing children this type of attachment in the natural world fosters empathy, kindness, and compassion in both their interpersonal and interspecies interactions.

An easy choice for the home, library, or classroom, our Beginnings collection has something to spark or sustain budding curiosity in any child.

Enjoy!

Dia

Dia L. Michels
Publisher, Platypus Media

P.S. Our supplemental learning materials enable adults to support young readers in their quest for knowledge. Check them out, free of charge, at PlatypusMedia.com.

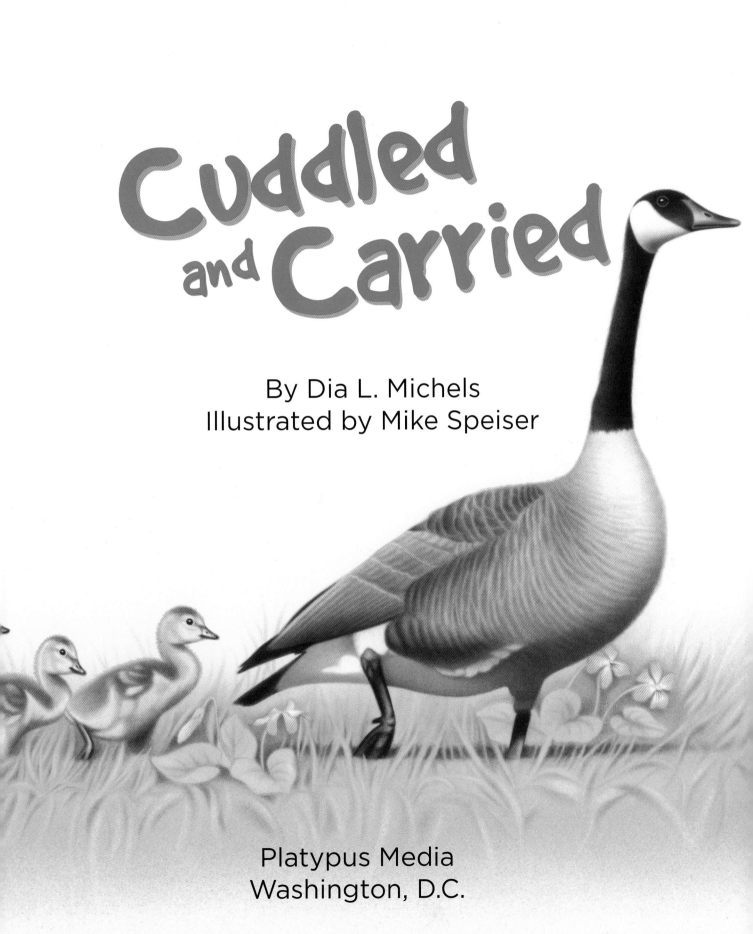

Cuddled and Carried

By Dia L. Michels
Illustrated by Mike Speiser

Platypus Media
Washington, D.C.

My mama grooms me

and guides me.

My mama cuddles me

and carries me.

My mama snuggles me

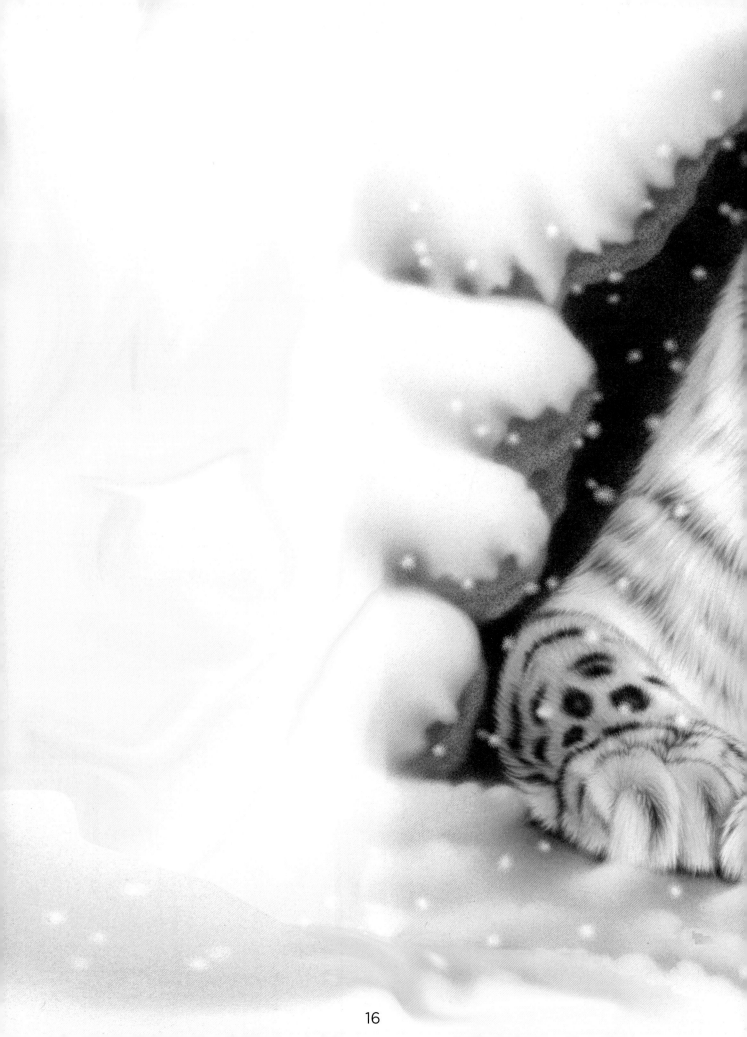

and shelters me.

My mama nurtures me

and nuzzles me.

My mama nourishes me.

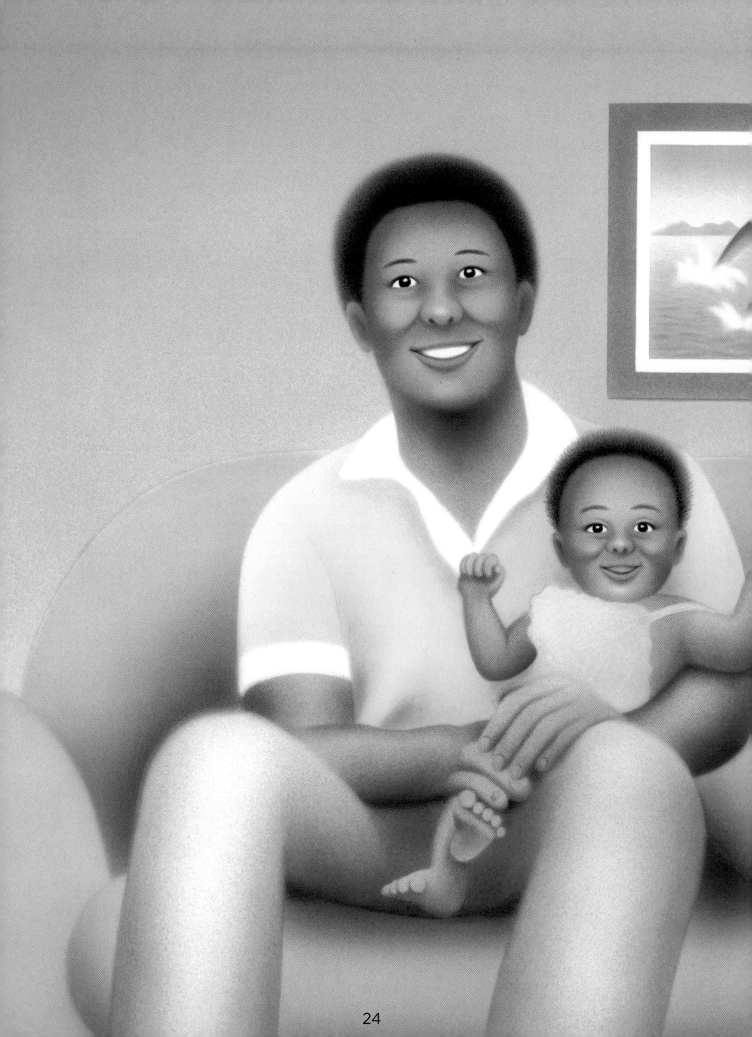

My family loves me very much.

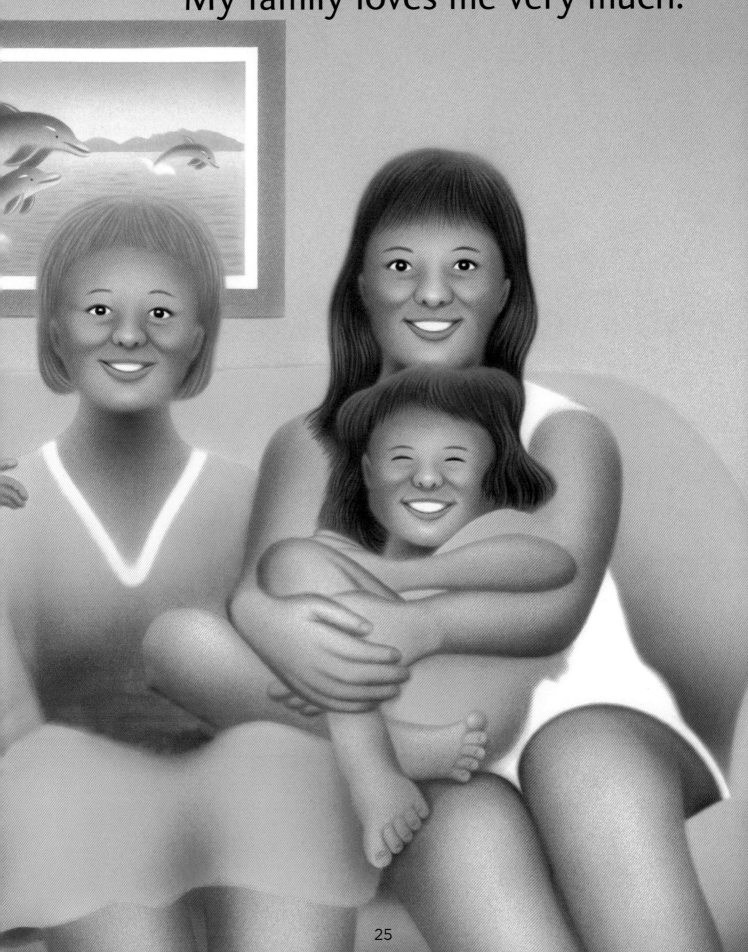

 Dia L. Michels is an internationally published, award-winning science and parenting writer who is committed to promoting attachment parenting. She has authored or edited over a dozen books for both children and adults. She can be reached at Dia@PlatypusMedia.com.

 Mike Speiser's artwork has been featured on the covers of *Wild Animal Baby* magazine and in the Leigh Yawkey Woodson Art Museum. He is involved with efforts to protect the natural world for future generations. He can be reached at Mike@PlatypusMedia.com.